# THE BLESSED TRINITY

This is a story about God, the Blessed Trinity. We say a special prayer and make a special sign to tell God we love Him.

JOHN AND MARY are saying the special prayer and making the special sign—the Sign of the Cross. They are saying, "In the Name of the Father, and of the Son, and of the Holy Spirit. Amen." We have a special name for God. The name is the Blessed Trinity. There is only one God. But there are three Persons in God. There is God the Father, and there is God the Son, and there is God the Holy Spirit.

WE'LL CALL this picture God the Father. God the Father is the first Person of the Blessed Trinity. But of course God the Father is really a spirit, and we cannot see a spirit. We draw God the Father as a man to help us think about Him. God the Father made this wonderful world and everyone and everything in it because He loves us *so* much.

GOD THE SON is sitting next to God the Father. God the Son is the second Person of the Blessed Trinity. Ever since the first Christmas, we call God the Son *Jesus*. Sometimes we call God the Son *the Sacred Heart*. That is why the Heart of Jesus shows in this picture. Jesus, God the Son, came to earth and died on the Cross for love of us. He opened the gates of Heaven, and He leads us to God the Father in Heaven.

THE THIRD PERSON of the Blessed Trinity is called God the Holy Spirit. Once, long ago, when Jesus was still on earth, God the Holy Spirit showed Himself right over the head of Jesus. He looked like a bird, a dove. You cannot draw a picture of a spirit, but God thought a dove was a good way to picture the Holy Spirit. So we draw a picture of a dove to help us think about God the Holy Spirit. God the Holy Spirit fills us with grace and love and teaches us how to be Saints.

SO THERE are three different Persons in the Blessed Trinity: God the Father, God the Son, and God the Holy Spirit. But there is only one God. The Blessed Trinity is *one* God. The Father, Son and Holy Spirit love one another very, very much. The three Persons in God are very, very happy.

THIS IS a picture of the Finley family. There are many persons in the Finley family: Papa Finley, Mama Finley and Ned Finley, Dorothy Finley, Peter Finley and baby Agnes. They are all different persons, but they are one family.

ALL THE PERSONS in the Finley Family love one another. They have such good times together. They are very happy.

NED FINLEY got a cocker spaniel puppy for his birthday. He named it Bounce. Ned is so happy that he is calling the neighbors: "Come on over, everyone, see my new puppy! Come and play with Bounce!" Ned was so happy with his puppy that he wanted to share it with his friends.

WHEN MOTHER had *her* birthday, Daddy brought her a big box of candy. "Oh, thank you, Daddy!" said Mother. "Everybody, come and have some of my candy!" Mother was so happy about her birthday present that she wanted to share her treat with everyone.

AT EASTER, Daddy Finley bought a big, shiny new car. It was a lovely color. "Hi, everybody!" said Dad. "Come out and see what I have for you!" He took the family for a ride. He was so happy with his big, shiny new car that he wanted to share it with everyone.

And that is how God is with us. God wants to share His goodness with everyone in the whole world.

NOW CLOSE your eyes and think of the Blessed Trinity living in your soul–God the Father, God the Son and God the Holy Spirit! God is listening. Whisper, "Thank You, dear God, for sharing Your goodness with me. I love You. Teach me to love You and please You always."

# PARTY FAVORS

Party favors, which may be used as place-cards, can easily be made from candy bars.

1) Wrap each candy bar in white paper.
2) Add a "book cover" from construction paper or cardboard.
3) Decorate the covers like books, with title and painted (or cut-out) decorations.

It is fun to have the title suggest the name of the child, and let the child guess which is his. Songs or nursery-rhymes or well-known stories make good titles. For instance, you could choose titles like:

"Mary had a Little Lamb,"
"Peter and the Wolf,"
"Jack and the Beanstalk," etc.

If how would you play you had no toys or games or books?

## KITCHEN MUSIC

When we were little, we were very lucky because we had a mother who understood that children sometimes have to be noisy. One can't always be noisy when one lives in a house with other people and next-door neighbors. But once in a while our mother let us make kitchen music.

We would each choose our own instrument. For instance, one of us might take an old cooking pot and a wooden spoon and use it for a drum. Someone else might take two pot lids to bang together. Some dried peas in a tin can made a fine rattle, and a funnel was just as good as a trumpet.

As soon as we had picked our instruments, Mother, who was the band leader, would line us up in single file. Sometimes we wore paper bags on our heads as uniforms. Someone gave the signal, and around the table we marched, singing and playing our ear-splitting kitchen music.

The funny thing about it was, that our music never lasted long. Somehow the noise inside us was used up very quickly, and we were almost relieved when our band leader gave the signal to stop. Then Mother invited us to a treat in the quiet kitchen.

# OF VOICES AND NOISES

When horses talk, we say they neigh.
But lions roar, and donkeys bray.
Pigs grunt, dogs bark, and roosters crow,
But when the cows say "Moo," they low.
Mice squeak, flies buzz, while grizzlies growl.
Lambs bleat –
And naughty children howl!

# SHEPHERD HONEST

(German Folktale)

Once there was a shepherd who had never told a lie. He was known as Shepherd Honest throughout the kingdom. At last even the King heard about him.

The King had a flock of sheep which was his pride and joy. A little white lamb was his special favorite. He would rather have lost his crown than this gentle little creature.

When the King heard of Shepherd Honest, he sent for him:

"I will make you the shepherd of my flock," he said to him. "Every day you shall come and give me a report about my sheep."

From that day on Shepherd Honest tended the King's sheep. Every day at noon he went to the palace. There he took off his hat before the King and waited for the same questions, to which he always gave the same answers:

"How are my sheep?"

"They are well as ever."

"How is my little white lamb?"

"It is playful and gentle and beautiful to behold."

This happened every day.

Now the King had an adviser who was false at heart. When he saw how much the King trusted the honest shepherd, he was afraid.

"I will lose my influence with the King," he thought, "unless I find a way to get rid of Shepherd Honest."

He went to the King.

"Your Majesty, I bet my head that Shepherd Honest will tell a lie before this week has passed."

The King would not believe him.

"I will bet my crown against your head," he answered, "that Shepherd Honest will never lie to me."

That night the false adviser told his wife about the bet. She laughed:

"I know of a way to make the shepherd tell a lie, just leave it to me! The King will lose his crown and we will be king and queen."

The following morning she dressed in her best finery and rode in a carriage to the place where Shepherd Honest tended his sheep. The poor shepherd had never seen a lady so beautiful. He hardly dared to look at her as she spoke:

"Dear Shepherd, I am in great distress and only you can save my life. For I must die this very day unless I eat the heart and liver of a little white lamb!" The shepherd's heart sank.

"Beautiful lady," he answered, "I would gladly give my life to save you, but the little white lamb belongs to the King. What would I tell him if it came to harm?"

"Tell him it fell off the cliff and broke its neck."

"I cannot tell a lie."

But the lady wept and pleaded until the shepherd could bear it no longer and killed the little white lamb. When she had eaten its fried heart and liver, the lady rode away.

The shepherd's heart was heavy as he walked to the King's palace. Every so often he stopped and rehearsed what he would say, speaking the King's part as well as his own.

"How are my sheep?"

"They are well as ever."

"How is my little white lamb?"

"Great grief has come, Your Majesty: the little lamb fell off a cliff and broke its little white neck."

Every time he said the lie, his heart ached. He walked slower and slower. When at last he reached the palace, the King and all his court awaited him in the throne room.

"How are my sheep?" began the King.

"They are well as ever."

"How is my little white lamb?"

The shepherd threw himself at the King's feet. "Great grief has come, Your Majesty! As I was tending the sheep today there came a lady, fair as an angel, and this she said to me: that she must die this very day unless she get the heart and liver of a little white lamb to eat. Forgive me, O King, I slaughtered the little white lamb!"

Then the King arose from his throne and lifted the shepherd from the ground.

"And if I have lost my little white lamb," he said, "I still have a man in my service who has never told a lie! Indeed, my crown is well protected."

The false adviser got what he deserved. Shepherd Honest stayed with the King and advised him in all matters and was held in great honor as long as he lived.